**Grumpy Bear**

**Best Friend Bear**

**Secret Bear**

This book belongs to: _____

**Wish Bear**

**Love-a-lot Bear**

Published by Scholastic Inc.
90 Old Sherman Turnpike, Danbury, CT 06816.

SCHOLASTIC and associated logos are trademarks and/or registered trademarks of Scholastic Inc.

ISBN 0-439-83582-8

First Scholastic Printing, May 2006

# Care Bears™ Friendship Club

# Best Friends Forever

by
Quinlan B. Lee

Illustrated by
Warner McGee

SCHOLASTIC INC.

New York   Toronto   London   Auckland   Sydney
Mexico City   New Delhi   Hong Kong   Buenos Aires

In Care-a-lot everyone loves to laugh and share
and show they care. Everyone is friends with each other.
But each Care Bear also has a perfect pal—who knows
and loves that Care Bear best—a best friend.

Wish Bear and Cheer Bear are best friends.
They love working together, as they cheer everyone on
to make their dreams come true.

GO Care Bears!

Secret Bear and Bashful Heart Bear are best
friends, too. They both love painting, roller-skating,

and finding secret hiding places.

Funshine Bear and Grumpy Bear love to read books, fly kites, and *juggle wishing stars.*

"Funshine Bear, we'll be best friends forever," said Grumpy Bear.

"And ever!"
Funshine Bear exclaimed.

13

One day, Grumpy Bear decided to go
for a balloon ride over the clouds. He couldn't
wait to ask Funshine Bear to go with him.

But when Grumpy Bear found Funshine Bear,
he was already playing hopscotch with Love-a-lot Bear
and Share Bear.

"I'm sorry, Grumpy Bear. I can't go on a balloon ride right now," Funshine Bear said.

"But I thought we were best friends," Grumpy Bear said, with a pout, and walked away.

17

Grumpy Bear sadly sat down on his favorite
cloud—right on top of Secret Bear!

"Why are you hiding in my favorite cloud?"
Grumpy Bear asked her.

"I wanted to fly kites with Bashful Heart Bear,
but he wanted to play by himself," replied Secret Bear.
"What good is a best friend who doesn't want to play?"

Best Friend Bear rode up on her bike.
"Did someone say *best friend*?" she asked.

"Our best friends won't play with us,"
said Secret Bear and Grumpy Bear.
"We thought best friends were forever."

"They are forever," said Best Friend Bear.
"But they aren't just for playing."

# "They aren't?"

Secret Bear and Grumpy Bear
asked together.

"Nope," Best Friend Bear said, smiling. "Best friends are for lots of things," Best Friend Bear added.

"They're the best at keeping secrets and for turning frowns upside down."

"It's just too bad our best friends can't play today,"
Secret Bear said, as a gust of wind blew past them.

"This wind is the best high-flying and
tail-waving kite wind ever!"
Secret Bear added.

"Why don't the three of us fly kites together?"
Best Friend Bear suggested. "I have some extra kites."

Secret Bear looked at Grumpy Bear and asked,
"Would you like to?"

"That sure would chase my grumps away,"
Grumpy Bear told Secret Bear.

"Does this mean that Funshine Bear isn't my best friend anymore?" Grumpy Bear wondered.

"Of course not," said Best Friend Bear.
"My tummy shows that best friends are *always*
connected. Friendship remains even when
friends are apart."

29

Secret Bear, Grumpy Bear, and Best Friend Bear
had a great time flying kites together. Best Friend Bear
even taught Secret Bear a kite-flying trick.

31

A little later, Funshine Bear and Bashful Heart Bear came looking for their best friends.

"I'm so glad to see you," said Grumpy Bear to Funshine Bear.

"I'm sorry I was grumpy with you. Do you forgive me?"

"Of course," Funshine Bear said.
"We're best friends, and best friends
are forever."

"Let's fly kites," Secret Bear said to Bashful Heart Bear. "Best Friend Bear just taught me a secret trick!"

"Why don't we take a ride in the hot air balloon now?" Grumpy Bear asked Funshine Bear.

# "Hooray!

# Friends are the best!"

shouted the five Care Bears together.

# How can you be a friend like Best Friend Bear?

Do you have a best friend?

❤ What do you like to do together?

Best Friend Bear said that best friends
are for more than just playing.
♥ Why is your best
   friend special to you?

Grumpy Bear and Secret Bear were upset when
their best friends couldn't play with them.
♥ Has that ever happened to you?
♥ Do best friends have to do everything together?

In the end, Grumpy Bear says he's sorry to Funshine Bear.
♥ Have you ever had to tell a friend that you were sorry?

Bashful Heart Bear

Cheer Bear

Share Bear

Bedtime Bear

Funshine Bear